I0520021

WORDS OF WISDOM

BOOK I

ALTON C. BROTHERS

WORDS OF WISDOM

BOOK I

Published by Alcliff Media Publishing

10 Waterside Plaza, Suite 19G

New York, New York 10010

© *2010 by Alton C. Brothers*

ISBN-10: 0615375529

ISBN-13: 9780615375526

LCCN: 2010908275

e-Store

www.createspace.com/3458533

ALL RIGHTS RESERVED

PREFACE

This book is a compilation of words of wisdom I have written over a period of more than thirty years. These words are the reflections of my life experiences as a participant and as an observer of others I encountered living each day.

The purpose of this book is to share these words of wisdom with you to bring you some type of enlightenment which will uplift or bring you encouragement in your daily living as you continue to live in this changing world.

Be thankful and happy that you woke up this morning. Give thanks to God because there are many people who did not wake up today. For life is not guaranteed to us each day.

Do that task right now and don't delay. It could be the difference between you achieving your goal and never getting another opportunity to succeed and prosper in your life.

Today, tell your wife that you love her because there is no guarantee that you will see her tomorrow. Let her know that she is a special part of your life.

Today, tell your children that you love them. This builds up their character and confidence as they try to find their way in this complex world.

Contemplation brings a
realization of self

Bringing forth the integral part
of your soul

Bringing you closer to the
infinite spiritual intangibles that
are not explainable at this
present time

Submit your ego to God so that
new and imaginable dreams
become a reality in your life some
day in the future.

Momentum

Thinking, planning, creating and enacting

This is what one must do to achieve a goal

As you start and go through the stages of achieving your dream and making it a reality

You gain nothing but momentum---that time when your can say

I have achieved my goal by being focused and continuing to stay on the course through a long struggle.

The more successful one is

The more envious people become because they never begin any goal of their own

For life can be a vicious cycle where people wear those disguised masks of deceit

However, the spiritual energy of God which is called faith can conquer all negativity around you

Continue your determination in achieving those goals of tomorrow

Remember to continue to fight

for those dreams and values you believe in

For one day, your dreams of today will become realities of tomorrow.

Success is only realized when
you have done your best and
gone the extra, extra mile

Continue the struggle to succeed
when others give up

You will be surprise what you
find at the end of your journey.

Today, be a blessing to someone
that you encounter in your
travels by saying a kind word
with a smile.

Remember, if something comes into your life too fast and you have not earned it, it will not last.

Freedom, freedom

Free spirit, free mind

Free time, free expression

Freedom is a child of creativity
and imagination.

Invest in yourself

For you should not do anything else

Invest money in something that will help you achieve the dream of owning a business

Go after your gold before its whereabouts are told

The secret of your treasure is in your soul.

Your health is your greatest wealth

Yes, some people take their physical wellbeing for granted

But there are those who wish that they had not neglected taking care of their bodies

The greatest wealth in the world is to be mentally and physically strong so you can strive and work towards reaching those stars above

Poor health has often changed the conditions in people's lives

These conditions could have been

avoided if they had listened to the advice of their inner spirit, to the advice of those who came before and who have lived a full life and to the advice of their physician when he said,

"Stop _____

For in this cavity lies man's greatest wealth.

Be patient and remember

Your dreams do not become a
reality by haste

But hold on to your faith in
yourself, work hard and lean on
the strength within your soul.

Anguish, determination, fatigue, hard work, follow-up, and frustration are all experienced in trying to become successful

Is it worth all the hassle?

Shall a flower bloom from the bud?

Time and patience can only tell.

Sooner or later

You shall find her

That special lady to love

An angel from above

One to make life's complexities
clear

Causing you to settle down and
stay

By her side as you build a life
together

Bringing happiness, love and
peace

This is an evolution of love.

A wedding has taken place

The union of two into one

Two sharing as well as caring

Two enjoying as well as crying

Two relinquishing their selfishness to make the other happy

A loving marriage can only be realized when two spiritually emerge as one spectrum of light.

Two who have been together for
a long time, grow tired and gray

They desire to get away from
each other

But once they go their own way

They realize they should go back
to their old ways and enjoy those
things they shared

Love, happiness and trust

Realizing that separation is
something that true lovers
should never have to pay.

Deep and true love shared by two is so unbearable when one partner is taken away by death

Just think, no more existence and sharing with that special mate that gave life breathe.

**Show the beauty and love in
your heart to all you meet today.**

Put God first in your life because
when you do he will always
guide you where you should be.

Today, tell those you care about that you appreciate them and you treasure their friendship.

Do what you say you are going to do because your actions show the world your true character and reveal the integrity of your words.

Just because someone tells you that it is free, it is not free.

Someone has paid for it or you will end up paying for it in some way.

Nothing is impossible for anyone
to obtain or to achieve

You are the artist who is
painting the masterpiece

Your talent is revealed by the
confidence, desire and faith to
create something new

Your masterpiece is never
completed because it is a
continuous process in which the
creative processes are never
finished

The masterpiece is extended
throughout your infinite life
experiences.

Think about helping others before helping yourself.

Where am I going?

What does the future hold for me?

What new adventure shall I encounter?

What shall I contribute to society to benefit all mankind?

Shall I contribute something new to the arts or the business world?

Shall I discover and learn the answers of untold secrets of life?

Time will only tell.

Forgive those who have wronged you and remove any strife from your heart about them and you will have internal peace.

If you keep strife in your heart, it will destroy you and make you miserable.

Do not become discouraged by today's disappointments

Focus on your goals, recognize your talents and employ discipline to use them correctly

Continue your quest for success and tomorrow your dream will become a reality

Consequently, your desire shall come forth as an endless ocean tide.

Successful but not satisfied

Patience has been a virtue I have been learning to master

I just continue to work diligently

Because of this long struggle, I appreciate mastering those negative forces which cause some to fail.

Flying above the earth in this airplane

Soul searching and trying to find new answers to unsolved problems

Soul searching is the fruition of the creative energy of my mind.

Confused by life's contradictions

Double standards make my head dizzy

Success or failure is a constant intimidator

However, one must keep pushing on for tomorrow

The future shall tell all those imposters to go to hell.

Success can only be obtained through hard work, patience and perseverance

One must work a lot longer then the average work day

Sometimes there will be sacrifices to be made

There will be times in which you must delay enjoyment

But eventually, your faith in yourself and patience will pay off

You will be glad that you continued to work towards your goal as few do

Pursuing a dream of yesterday and making it a reality today

True success is the ability to make an idea in your mind a reality in the world where people can see and benefit from your idea.

Boredom is what causes me to go home

Home to relax and listen to some good music alone

For my creativeness reveals itself when I listen to music and its bad tone

Ideas come to my mind

Come out on my paper on time

For music is my song

So shall the fortunes of my life be untold.

Face your problems realistically

Do not try to ignore what is truly there

Say that the problem is this_____

Think about how you plan to attack and eliminate this problem

Be honest with yourself about the problem and a truthful solution will develop

The spirit within the soul will reveal a true solution to your problem.

To give birth is to give light to the world

To give encouragement is to give unconditional love

To listen to one's problem is to give support when one is troubled

To encourage someone is to give new dreams a beginning.

Ladies do not become so desperate for a man that you are willing to reveal all your treasures too soon

For if the value of a treasure is revealed too soon, the value is never seen for its true essence.

Parents remember that you can tell your children what they should do, but the best way to instruct them is to live your life each day the way you tell them to live. Children will always act the way they see their parents act everyday in their lives. Your children want to be like you.

When someone has done something good for you, remember to tell them thanks in some way. This shows that you appreciated what they did. Remember, that person did not have to do what they did.

Watch what you say because words uttered have a power of their own that will produce results and will return to you some day.

Remember to respect those people who have come before you and have many life experiences that they might want to share with you to prevent you from going through some of the pains found in growing up.

They have wisdom which could keep you from finding out the hard way about what is real and not on television or in the movies.

If you are willing to stop and listen to what they say and not think you know everything, you might learn something.

At a standstill in my life

Successful but not satisfied

Impulse to venture and be free

I need to get into composing
songs

That's all I want to do

This is my present and only true
desire

To write million dollar songs

Expressing my talents in music
for all mankind

Rather than letting myself be
denied

Denied the opportunity of being free and making my dream come true.

Tired of present job

Must re-evaluate next spring

Successful but going nowhere is
how I feel.

Entrepreneurs never become complacent

They are always thinking about new ideas and discovering something not seen by the naked eye.

Remember that the world owes you nothing. You have to make your way in this world by working to obtain your dreams.

You must take the action to discover the unknown mysteries in your life. You must walk the path that God has given you if you listen what is inside your soul. It is not what people tell you what they think you should do. It is what is in your heart that you must do. Only you know the truth about yourself.

A new beginning

Letting go of the past starting anew

Seeking the miracles at the end of your life's rainbow

Start the day with a new thought.

As you go through your life battles

Remember that God is always there beside you

He is in you

He is around you

So never feel alone in your battlefields.

The actions that you do reveal
what is in your heart

And tell the world about your
true character.

Remember that one does not get respect because of a title or position, but by how one lives his life everyday

Your true character is revealed each day by the way you treat people

True respect is not given but is earned.

When offering your services to someone, make sure that you get a written contract before you start your work. By doing this, no one can say that they do not remember those things that you discussed and agreed to provide your client. In business, one's words are not enough to make sure that you are compensated for those services you provide a client. Your work has value and you must remember that you are not giving all your hard work away free.

Remember to be on time for any appointment because time is valuable and successful people do not have time to waste. By being on time you present yourself as one who is serious about your purpose in the eyes of the person with whom you have the appointment. It could be the difference between you getting a great opportunity to prosper in your business and never getting the opportunity at all.

Where am I going?

What shall tomorrow bring?

Shall I encounter a new positive experience?

Or shall I continue and find my destiny?

Remember

You may deceive, lie or mislead someone but the truth always has a way of revealing itself when you do not expect it.

Wondering how long it shall be before I can do the things that I imagine and mentally see?

How long shall this quest burn in my heart, soul and mind?

It's nothing but a matter of time before all is released by God

My dream of becoming a

_____

will become a reality that the world will see.

ABOUT THE AUTHOR

Alton C. Brothers has been using his writing talents since his childhood by composing philosophical words, poems, and songs when he was growing up in Norfolk, Virginia. However, after graduating from Morehouse College in Atlanta, Georgia, he continued writing in private and utilized his writing talents in the U. S. Coast Guard and in the business world when he worked for Fortune 500 companies in the areas of advertising, human resources, marketing and sales over a period of more than thirty years.

Recently, God told Alton to put

all the "words of wisdom" that he had written over this time period in a book to share with people living today in this changing world. The results of all these words are in this book, "Words of Wisdom, Book I.

In addition, Alton is an award winning fine art photographer and some of his works are owned by a former ambassador, celebrities, and others who collect fine art photography. Alton's work can be seen on his website---
www.altonbrothersphotos.com.

www.ingramcontent.com/pod-product-compliance
Lightning Source LLC
Chambersburg PA
CBHW071347130626
46556CB00005B/2068